Poodles look serious but love to play

Poodles

Anne Fitzpatrick

Smart Apple Media

🐏 Published by Smart Apple Media

1980 Lookout Drive, North Mankato, MN 56003

Designed by Rita Marshall

Printed in the United States of America

🐏 Photographs by Barbara Augello, Corbis (Robert Dowling), Kent & Donna Dannen, Tom Myers

🐏 Library of Congress Cataloging-in-Publication Data

Fitzpatrick, Anne. Poodles / by Anne Fitzpatrick.

p. cm. — (Dog breeds) Summary: Introduces the physical characteristics, breeding, training, and care of the popular pet and glamorous show dog. Includes a recipe for poodle-shaped cookies.

🐏 ISBN 1-58340-314-0

1. Poodles—Juvenile literature. [1. Poodles. 2. Dogs.] I. Title. II. Series.

SF429.P85 F48 2003   636.72'8—dc21   2002042627

🐏 First Edition 9 8 7 6 5 4 3 2 1

Poodles

CONTENTS

Poodle Fashion

Everybody knows a poodle when he or she sees one. The poodle's long, narrow nose, fluffy ears, and dainty body are easy to recognize. Yet poodles can come in just about any color—white, black, brown, red, cream, gray, silver, **apricot**, and even pink or blue! Most poodles are just one color, but there are some that are two colors. Poodles also come in three very different sizes. The tiny toy poodle is about eight inches (20 cm) from the top of its shoulder to the ground.

Poodles are among the most intelligent dogs

It barely reaches an adult's knee. The miniature poodle ranges from 10 to 15 inches (25–38 cm) tall at the shoulder. The standard poodle is the largest. It measures 21 to 26 inches (53–66 cm). It could lick a first-grader's face without jumping up! Poodles are famous for their fancy haircuts. The most well-known poodle cut is called the

Tiny "teacup" poodles are even smaller than toy poodles; they can weigh as little as two pounds (1 kg)!

Continental trim. The face, behind, legs, and tail of the dog are shaved. Pompoms, or puffs, of hair are left at the ankles and on

A standard poodle with a Continental trim

A group, or litter, of standard poodle puppies

the end of the tail. The hair on the head and upper body is left

long and fluffy. Some people think the haircut makes the dog

look like a lion.

Oodles of Poodles

Standard poodles usually have **litters** of six to eight

puppies. Some litters may have as many as 14 puppies! Toy and

miniature poodles have smaller litters of about four puppies. A

female poodle is pregnant for just three months before giving

birth to her litter. Toy and miniature poodles grow up

faster than standard poodles. Toy poodle puppies reach their

adult size at seven months old. Miniature poodles are full-

grown at one year, and standard poodles at one and a half to

two years. Although the smaller dogs grow up faster, they often behave more like puppies, even into old age. Most poodles live between 10 and 18 years. Some poodles have been known to live as long as 21 years. The smaller dogs usually live longer. All three kinds of poodles continue to be very active and playful as they age.

A Working Dog

Today, the poodle is a glamorous **show dog** and popular pet. But long ago, poodles were working dogs. They were trained to **retrieve** ducks and other animals shot by their hunting masters. Their sleek bodies made them good

swimmers, and their thick, wooly hair kept them warm even

when wet. Fancy poodle haircuts started out as a way to make

it easier for the dogs to swim, while leaving some hair to keep

A poodle getting ready for a dog show

them warm. Smaller versions of the poodle were the much-loved favorites of kings and queens in 18th-century Europe. Queen Anne of England was delighted by two miniature poodles dancing to-gether. Poodles have long been popular circus dogs because of their ability to stand and move on their hind legs. They are also very easy to train.

Other dog breeds have been crossed with poodles to create the Cockerpoo, Schnoodle, Labradoodle, and Pekepoo.

Apricot poodles have wooly, light brown hair

Poodles as Pets

The poodle's bright, loving personality has made it a popular pet. Its gentle good nature and ability to learn have made it a very practical pet as well. **Some people think that black poodles are the best-behaved poodles, while apricot poodles are the worst behaved.** Poodles are very good with young chil-dren. The standard poodle is especially easygoing and calm. However, when its family is threatened, the poodle is an excellent guard dog. All three sizes of poodle are loyal and fearless. Even the tiny toy poodle will bark to defend its owner's property! Poodles

do not **shed**, which keeps the house clean but means that they

need a haircut every month or two. Their thick coats need

daily brushing. As with any pet, it is important to think about

Poodles of all sizes are loyal, loving pets

the time and money needed to take good care of a poodle.

Poodles are very energetic dogs. They need daily walking and a lot of playtime. Poodle puppies need extra time and care to train, as well as many trips to the **veterinarian** for checkups.

It was once popular to allow a poodle's hair to grow down to the ground in long, rope-like cords.

Throughout the years, poodles have been hunting dogs, circus entertainers, show dogs, and beloved family pets. The poodle has truly been man's and woman's best friend!

Some people still use poodles as hunting dogs

A Yummy Haircut

Designing a poodle's fancy haircut can be fun—and tasty! Be sure to have an adult help you with this activity.

What You Need

Tracing paper

A pencil

Scissors

A rolling pin

Refrigerated sugar cookie dough

Colored sugar, icing, candies, and nuts

A dull knife

Cookie sheets

An oven

What You Do

1. Trace the poodle on the opposite page.
2. Cut out the poodle outline.
3. Roll out the cookie dough until it is about 1/4 inch (.5 cm) thick.
4. Lay your outline on the dough and trace around it with a dull knife. Make as many poodles as you can. Put the poodles on cookie sheets after you cut them out.
5. Give your poodles different haircuts using the colored sugar, icing, candies, and nuts.
6. Have an adult help you bake them. Then eat up!

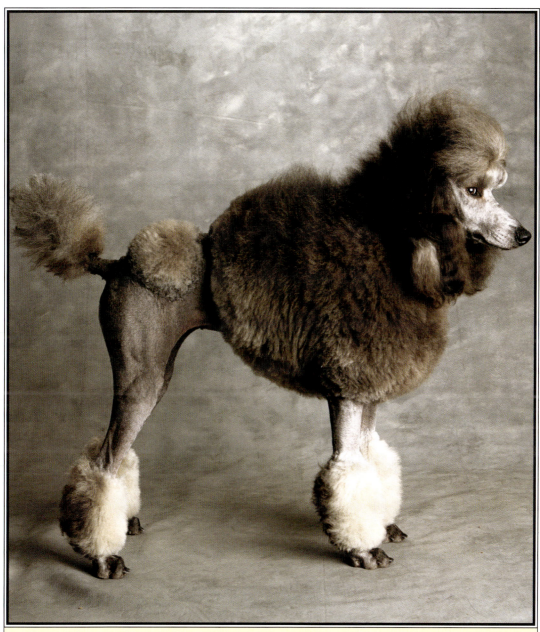

A poodle's coat can be a work of art

INFORMATION

Index

Words to Know

apricot (AP-ri-kot)—a yellowish-orange color

litters (LITT-urz)—groups of puppies born at the same time

retrieve (re-TREEV)—to find and bring something back

shed (SHED)—to lose hair a little at a time

show dog (SHO dog)—a dog that competes with other dogs in contests

veterinarian (VET-ur-eh-NAIR-ee-en)—a doctor for animals

Read More

Dunbar, Ian. *The Essential Poodle*. New York: John Wiley & Sons, 1999.

Fogle, Bruce. *Dog Breed Handbooks: Poodle*. New York: DK Publishing, 1999.

Zolotow, Charlotte. *The Poodle Who Barked at the Wind*. New York: Henry Holt, 2001.

Internet Sites

American Kennel Club: Poodle

http://www.akc.org/breeds/recbreeds/poodle.cfm

The Poodle History Project

http://www.poodlehistory.org

The Poodle Club of America

http://www.poodleclubofamerica.org